W9-BZY-423

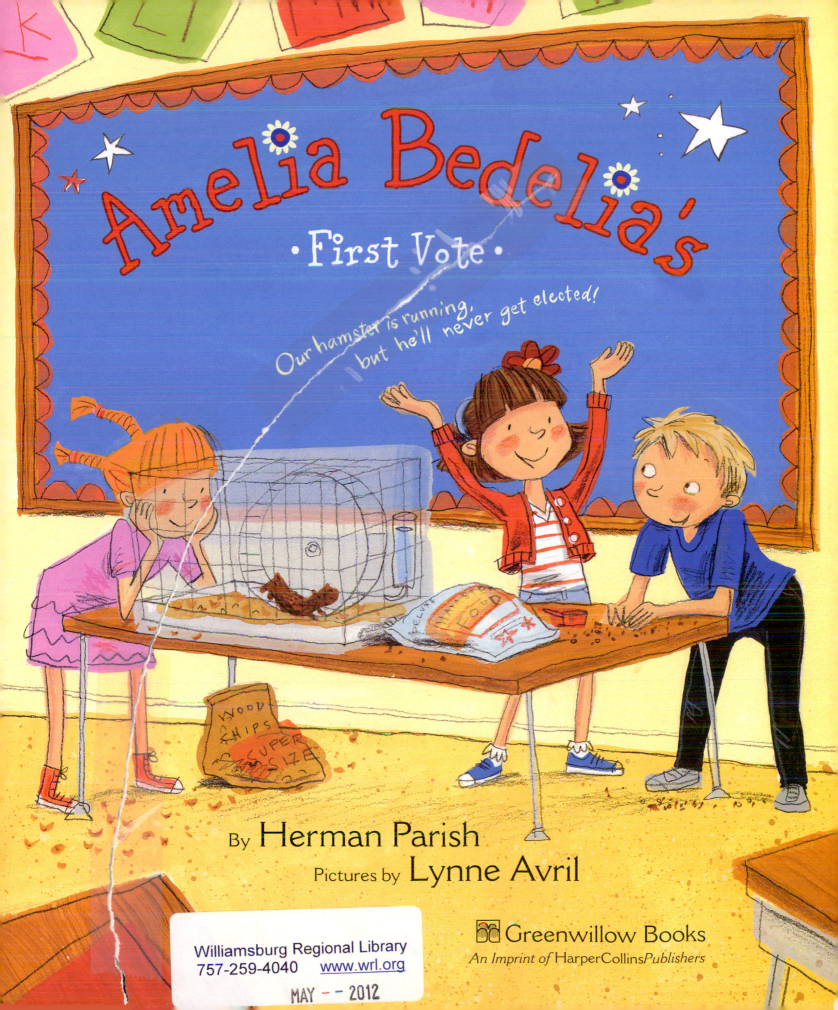

Amelia Bedelia's

• First Vote •

Our hamster is running, but he'll never get elected!

By Herman Parish

Pictures by Lynne Avril

Greenwillow Books

An Imprint of HarperCollinsPublishers

Rosemary gets my vote! — H. P.

Chloe gets my vote
for Best Mom! — L.A.

Today!
Elections

Amelia Bedelia's First Vote. Text copyright © 2012 by Herman S. Parish III
Illustrations copyright © 2012 by Lynne Avril
Amelia Bedelia is a registered trademark of Peppermint Partners, LLC.
All rights reserved. Manufactured in China.
For information address HarperCollins Children's Books, a division of HarperCollins Publishers,
10 East 53rd Street, New York, NY 10022. www.harpercollinschildrens.com
Gouache and black pencil were used to prepare the full-color art. The text type is Cantoria MT.
Library of Congress Cataloging-in-Publication Data: Parish, Herman.
Amelia Bedelia's first vote / by Herman Parish ; illustrated by Lynne Avril. p. cm.
"Greenwillow Books." Summary: When Amelia Bedelia runs into her principal, Mr. K,
and plants the idea that students should vote on the rules, he decides that her class should
be the first to come up with new ideas for running the school.
ISBN 978-0-06-209405-6 (trade bdg.) — ISBN 978-0-06-209406-3 (lib. bdg.)
[1. Politics, Practical—Fiction. 2. Schools—Fiction.] I. Avril, Lynne, (date) ill. II. Title.
PZ7.P2185Ap 2012 [E]—dc23 2011028546

12 13 14 15 16 SCP First Edition 10 9 8 7 6 5 4 3 2 1   Greenwillow Books

Amelia Bedelia loved going to school because every day was an adventure.

"Bravo! You are all here," said Miss Edwards one morning.

She handed the attendance sheet to Amelia Bedelia.

"Please take the attendance for me, Amelia Bedelia."

"But why?" asked Amelia Bedelia.
"Didn't you just take it?"
Miss Edwards smiled. "Take
the attendance to the office,"
she said, "so they will know that
no one is sick."
"Wait," said Cliff. "I'm very sick.
Sick of school!"

Everyone laughed, except
Amelia Bedelia.
"Should I mark Cliff as sick?"
she asked.
"No," said Miss Edwards.
"Cliff will be cured soon.
We're going to learn all about
elections today. We'll even
vote! But we won't start
without you, so hurry back."

Amelia Bedelia raced out of the classroom. "Slow down!" called Miss Edwards. "And say hello to Mr. K if you run into him."

Amelia Bedelia walked properly
until Miss Edwards was out of sight.
Then she began to run again.

She hoped she would see Mr. K. He
was the principal. His real name was
hard to say, so he told everyone
to call him
Mr. K.

Amelia Bedelia's sneakers screeched
on the floor like the tires of a car. She smiled
down at her feet. KABLAM! The next thing
she saw was stars.

"Uh, hi, Mr. K," said Amelia Bedelia.
"Are you hurt?" asked Mr. K.
"I'm okay," said Amelia Bedelia,
but when she tried to stand up,
she was as wobbly as a baby lamb.

"Hmmm," said Mr. K. "Let
me take you to the office."

This was Amelia Bedelia's first trip
to the principal's office. She really
wished she hadn't been running
in the hall.

Luckily, Mr. K took Amelia Bedelia to the nurse's
office instead.
"My goodness," said Nurse Simms. "Where did you run
into Amelia Bedelia?"
"Actually, I ran into him," said Amelia Bedelia.
"She's a bit dizzy," said Mr. K. "Will you check her out?"

"Why were you running?" asked Nurse Simms.

"We're having an election," said Amelia Bedelia.

"I see," said Nurse Simms. "What are you running for?"

"The office," said Amelia Bedelia.

"Of course," said Nurse Simms. "Which office?"

"That one," said Amelia Bedelia, pointing toward the school office.

"How is she doing?" asked Mr. K a few minutes later.

"She is in the pink," said Nurse Simms.

"With purple stripes," said Amelia Bedelia.

"Wow!" said Mr. K. "Those stripes will match that bruise on your knee. Now you can see why we don't allow running in the halls."

"I am sorry," said Amelia Bedelia. "Am I in trouble?"

"Well," said Mr. K, "what would you do if you were me?"

Amelia Bedelia looked Mr. K over from head to toe.

"If I were you, I would wear happier ties," she said.

Mr. K smiled. "I meant, what rules would you make?" he said.

At that moment, Miss Edwards
rushed into the office.
"Amelia Bedelia!" she said. "There
you are! Let's walk back to class
together. Everyone is eager to vote."
Suddenly, Amelia Bedelia had an idea.
"Mr. K!" she said.
"Now I know what I would do if
I were you. I would let the kids
vote on the rules!"

"Amelia Bedelia," said Mr. K,
"I think you've got something."
Amelia Bedelia felt her forehead.
"No," she said. "Nurse Simms said
I was fine."

"You are absolutely fine," said Mr. K, "and so is your idea. Why don't you have your class come up with a few new ideas for running the school? And I promise to do whatever gets the most votes."

When the class heard about Mr. K's promise,
they cheered and hollered and jumped
up and down.
Miss Edwards clapped her hands.
"Cupcakes," she said. "It is important
that your voices be heard,
but not by the whole town."

Kids rule the school! Hooray! Hooray!

Amelia Bedelia for Principal!!

"Now," said Miss Edwards, when the room had settled down.
"We need a list of ideas to vote on. This will be our ballot.
Raise your hand when you think of something."
Everyone was quiet, and then . . .

"I'd like more ice cream for dessert," said Joy.

"I want sandwiches for lunch," said Pat.

"Hey!" said Clay. "How about . . . ice cream sandwiches for lunch!"

Angel said, "Let's plant berry bushes in the school garden for healthy snacks and . . ."

"Let's grow popcorn!" yelled Teddy.

"It is rude to interrupt," said Miss Edwards. "Remember to raise your hand if you'd like the floor."

Amelia Bedelia raised both hands.
"I'd like the floor and the ceiling," she said.
A few kids giggled, but she was serious.
"We get too much homework," she said.
"I wish we could have one night without it.
Then I could have more fun with my mom
and dad."

"I'd ride my bike,"
said Skip.

"I could play
my piano,"
said Heather.

"I know," said Penny. "Let's call
it Homework-Free Wednesdays!"

HOORAY!

"Hooray!" yelled the whole class.
They all liked that idea a lot.

At the end of the day, Miss Edwards gave every student a copy of the ballot. "We'll vote tomorrow, chickadees," she said, "so be sure to sleep on it tonight."

☐ Ice cream sandwiches for lunch
☐ Grow berries in school garden
☐ Homework-Free Wednesdays
☐ Kids read morning announcements
☐ Class trip to the circus
☐ Bring stuffed animals to school
☐ Fish tank in every room
☐ Stoplights at hall intersections

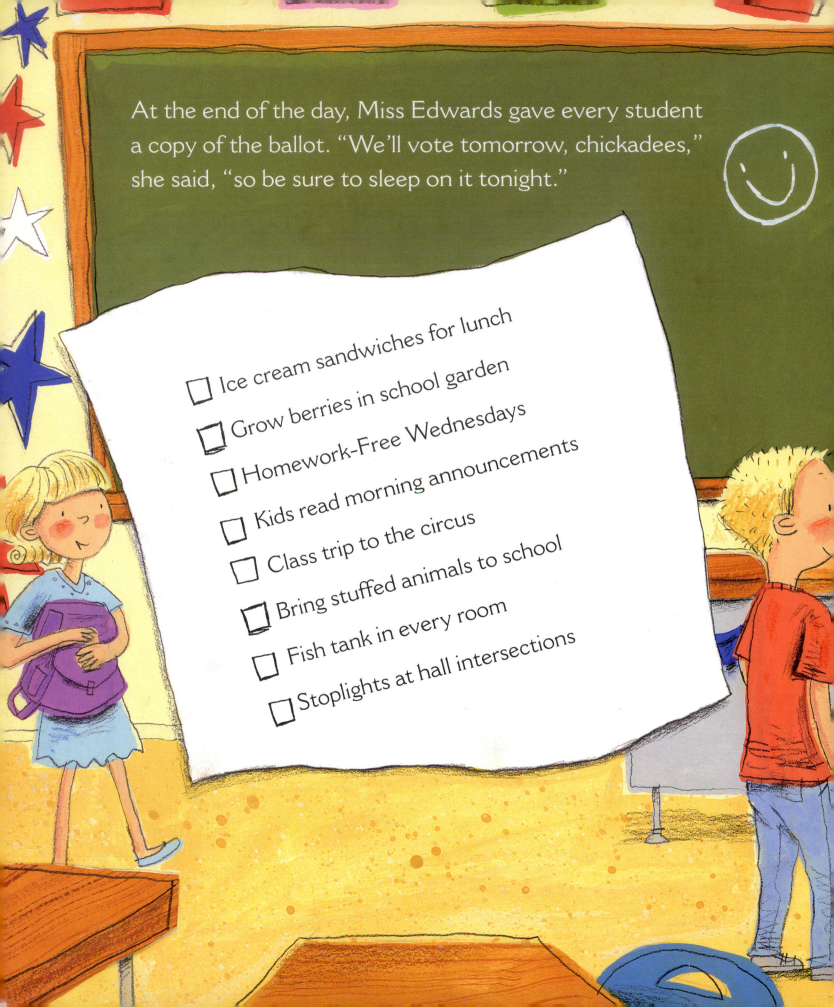

The next morning, Miss Edwards took attendance as usual.
"Wade is on a trip with his parents, and Dawn is out sick," she said.
"That leaves fourteen of you to vote."
Amelia Bedelia took out her ballot.
She wished she hadn't slept so hard on it.

Ice cream sandwiches for lunch
~~Grow berries in school garden~~
Homework - Free Wednesdays
~~Kids read morning announcements~~
~~Class trip to the circus~~
~~Bring stuffed animals to school~~
~~Fish tank in every room~~
~~Stoplights at hall intersections~~

Everyone voted. They counted the votes, and then Miss Edwards crossed out the idea that got the fewest votes. They voted and counted again, and again Miss Edwards crossed out the idea with the smallest number of votes. They kept doing this until just two ideas were left.

"Okay, my chipmunks," said Miss Edwards. "This is your last vote. How many want ice cream sandwiches for lunch?"
Seven kids raised their hands.

Then she asked, "How many want Wednesdays to be homework-free?"
Seven different hands went up.

"Gracious," said Miss Edwards. "It is seven to seven.
We need a recount."
They voted again. Again it was seven to seven.
"We have a tie," said Miss Edwards.
"What kind of tie?" asked Amelia Bedelia.

"The election is tied," said Miss Edwards.
"Each idea got the same number of votes."
"What do we do now?" asked Teddy.

"The same thing we do every day," said Miss Edwards.
"It's time for recess! Then we'll have a runoff to determine
the winner."
That sounded like fun, especially to Amelia Bedelia.
Everyone raced to the playground.

"When we go back inside,"
said Clay to Amelia Bedelia,
"I'll beat you in the runoff, for sure."
"There's no running in school,"
said Amelia Bedelia. "Let's
run off right now. I'll race you
around the building."

"On your marks," said Angel.
"Get set," said Cliff.
"Go!" hollered Rose.
Clay and Amelia Bedelia took off.

"Go, Clay!" shouted Joy.
"Hug the corners,
Amelia Bedelia!" yelled Skip.

Amelia Bedelia was way ahead at the first turn,
but then she stopped to hug the corner.
Clay whooped as he passed her.

Amelia Bedelia ran even harder.

She passed Clay in a burst of speed,

but hugging every corner slowed her down.

They were running neck and neck at the finish line.

Just then, Miss Edwards walked outside. "It's time for our runoff, squirrels and ladybugs—"

KABLAM!!

"Amelia Bedelia," said Nurse Simms, "you brought me two
new patients."
"I didn't know a runoff could be so rough," said Amelia Bedelia.
Mr. K shook his head. "That runoff was more like a run over,"
he said. "This is turning into the School of Hard Knocks."

"Knock, knock," said a woman at the door. "I'm Dawn's mother. She was sick today and I came to get her homework and to give you this."

Miss Edwards opened the note from Dawn and read it aloud.

Dear Miss Edwards,
I'm sorry I missed the election.
I'm feeling better.
I vote for: Homework Free
~~Wendsdays~~ :)
Wednesdays
Bye for now.
Dawn

"Wow!" said Miss Edwards. "I need to show Dawn's note
to the class. This is what we call an absentee ballot.
It lets your vote count, even if you can't be there."
"Hey," said Clay, "that means there isn't a tie after all."
"That's right," said Miss Edwards. "Dawn cast the swing vote."

Amelia Bedelia felt like swinging from the ceiling.
"Hooray!" she yelled. "Homework-Free Wednesdays wins!"
"Congratulations, Amelia Bedelia," said Mr. K. "Do you have anything to add?"
"I will when we do arithmetic," said Amelia Bedelia.
"But right now I really do like your new tie."

"Thank you, Amelia Bedelia," said Mr. K.
"It's great to have your vote."